Get Fit with Nelson

SIMON WESTON
in collaboration with David FitzGerald

Illustrated by
Jac Jones

Pont

Published in 2013 by Pont Books, an imprint of
Gomer Press, Llandysul, Ceredigion, SA44 4JL

ISBN 978 1 84851 713 4
A CIP record for this title is available from the British Library.

This book is published with the financial support of the
Welsh Books Council.

Printed and bound in Wales at
Gomer Press, Llandysul, Ceredigion

Chapter One

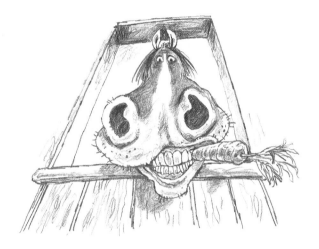

Welcome back! And, if you haven't been to my stable before, welcome!

Things are pretty much the same at the St Mary Dairy in Pont-y-cary, although some of the permanent residents aren't *quite* what they used to be! I'll tell you more about that in a minute. Some things don't change, of course. Flight Lieutenant Pigeon, the carrier pigeon with no sense of direction is as dizzy as ever, and Cardigan, the ex-racehorse, still dozes most of the time, perhaps even more than he used to.

James Pond, the frog in the bow tie who thinks he's a special agent, still runs spying operations from the pool but the All Quacks, the rugby-playing ducks led by Sir Francis Drake, manage to keep an eye on him. So...all pretty normal really! Mad.

I thought things couldn't get much more complicated after our trip to Tenby, but let me tell you about what happened a few weeks ago. I was listening to my favourite presenter, the lovely Brecon, on my favourite radio station, *Hoarse FM* – the home of equine entertainment. Brecon used to be a pop star – with a backing group called the Spice Foals. Now she plays the best music and organises some great competitions. And I think she is lovely...but don't tell anyone.

Anyway, I had just finished breakfast. Three bags of oats, two carrots and an apple. Very nice. Flight Lieutenant Pigeon was up in the rafters, wiping his beak after eating some seed and a small piece of bread. The All Quacks had been snacking on pondweed, and James Pond, the lunatic frog, had just had a 'full English fly-up', as he calls it...which was just a big plate of flies really. I try to tell him it's a 'full Welsh' breakfast but old habits die hard.

Everyone was happy and well fed. Even my boss, Mike the Milk, had given me a cheery wave as he cleared his breakfast things into the bin. Only Rhodri and Rhys, the ridiculous rats, were missing. They normally had their breakfast *near* that same bin...though sometimes they had their breakfast *in* it.

But all was very quiet until, suddenly, Rhys came running into the stable. He burst in, gasping for air, and pointing in the direction he'd come from. 'Rhodri...' he squeaked, 'stuck...pipe...too...small...'

'What?' I said, looking out into the yard.

'Rhodri...pipe...' he wheezed and ran out. Well, when I say *ran* out, he *wobbled* out. Both he and his brother have put on quite a bit of weight recently.

Anyway, Rhys scampered across the yard to the back door of Mike the Milk's kitchen. I trotted along behind. It was then that I saw them. A pair of legs dangling from the overflow drainpipe, tiny toes wiggling in the wind.

'Help!' came a muffled cry from inside the pipe.

'What are you doing, you ridiculous rat?'

'Someone made the pipe smaller,' cried Rhodri.

'Rubbish,' I said. 'What were you doing in the pipe anyway?'

'I was going to have my shower; it's that time of year again,' said Rhodri.

I think I should explain that comment. Rhodri and Rhys are real rats. They have real rat habits. Eating from bins, never using a toothbrush, burping out loud and having one shower a year...in an overflow drainpipe...that's their normal behaviour.

By now, Rhodri was beginning to whimper. 'Get me out...please.'

The whole dairy had heard the commotion and had gathered by the back door, even Mike. He was now standing in the doorway.

'There's a rat wedged up your drainpipe,' I said.

'Mmmmm,' said Mike, rubbing his chin. 'Well, he can't stay there. There's nothing worse than a blocked pipe. That's my overflow from the bath.'

'I know,' I sighed. 'He was using it as a shower.'

'Oh,' said Mike. 'That time of year again; it comes round so quickly.'

'Can we undo the pipe?' I asked.

Mike started to fiddle with the bolts which held the pipe in place and within a matter of moments the drainpipe was free but, sadly, Rhodri wasn't. He was still jammed inside.

Mike shook the pipe.

'Wooooowoooooo!' shouted Rhodri.

Mike thought for a moment, then tapped the pipe against the wall.

'Ow! Ow! Ow!'

Finally Mike gave Rhodri's legs a little tug, but nothing happened. The rat was stuck fast.

'Mmmmmm,' said Mike. 'I wonder. What about some butter?'

'Yes please,' came the voice from inside the pipe.

'What?'

'Some toast would be nice as well. Maybe a bit of jam?' suggested Rhodri.

'No . . . no . . . no,' I said.

Rhys laughed. 'Don't be ridiculous, Rhodri.'

'Exactly,' I said. 'At last a sensible comment.'

'You wouldn't be able to get a piece of toast down the drainpipe,' said Rhys. 'It would be too wide.'

'You could get French bread down there,' added one of the All Quacks.

'We love French bread,' chorused his mates.

'Spaghetti,' said Rhodri. 'You could get spaghetti down a drainpipe!'

'And a banana,' added Rhys. 'Mind you, it would have to be a straight one.'

'I like straight bananas,' said Rhodri from the pipe. 'They taste all . . . straighty.'

'Straighty . . . straighty! That's not even a word,' I objected, but nobody was listening to me.

'An éclair,' said Rhys. 'Have you got an éclair?'

'Look,' I shouted. 'We haven't come to feed Rhodri; we're here to free Rhodri. And he is stuck for a reason. It's because he's put on weight. The pipe hasn't got smaller; Rhodri's got bigger. So, no spaghetti, no French bread, no éclairs and no bananas, straighty or not.'

'So why the butter?' asked Rhys.

Mike looked down the pipe. 'If we butter the inside it might help him slide out. Hang on. I'll go and get some.'

Mike vanished into his kitchen and came back with the butter dish. He buttered Rhodri's legs, he buttered the inside of the pipe, he buttered both the ends and he even dropped some butter down so that Rhodri could butter himself.'

'Thank you,' said Rhodri.

'Don't eat it!' I shouted.

'Awwww,' said Rhodri.

The All Quacks and Sir Francis Drake took hold of his legs.

Mike gripped the other end of the pipe. 'Right,' he said. 'When I say pull, you pull. One, two, three . . . PULL!'

Well, I thought Mike had used too much butter and I was right. The All Quacks ended up in a heap of feathers; Mike lost his grip and crashed through the kitchen door; but the pipe, with Rhodri still in it, just rolled about uselessly on the floor.

I sat there and folded my hooves. It was going to be a long day.

Welcome to the St Mary Dairy at Pont-y-cary. Where buttered-rat-tugging is the latest sport.

Chapter Two

While everybody else was picking themselves up and wiping butter from their hands, paws and wings, I lifted up the pipe with my hoof and put an eye to the end, the end that was rat-free.

'Right,' I said. 'Things have got to change. You have got to lose some weight, get fit and stop using Mike's drainpipe as a shower. OK?'

'OK,' echoed a sad little voice. 'I promise but please get me out.'

Mike was now standing beside me. 'How much puff have you got?'

'Puff?'

'Puff,' he repeated. 'Can you put your mouth to the pipe and blow?'

What a great idea! Mike is smart like that. So, taking a deep breath, I summoned up all my puff and...blew.

POP! Out flew Rhodri – across the yard and straight into the pond. SPLASH! He was free.

Now, here's a bit of advice. If you're ever going to use a rat and drainpipe like a pea-shooter, always look at where you're firing it.

Rhodri struggled out of the water, looking the very picture of . . . a drowned rat.

'What a shame!' sniggered Rhys. 'And just after his shower. Fancy getting wet twice in one year . . . Eeukk.'

After rubbing Rhodri in a towel and hanging bits of him up to dry, we all sat in the stable for a little chat.

'Rhodri,' I said. 'You need to lose some weight.'

Rhys laughed. 'Fat rat . . . fat rat . . . fat rat . . .'

'Now that is not nice,' I said. 'Calling people names is nasty and besides . . . I have to say that you've put some weight on too. You're just as round as your brother.'

Rhys's whiskers drooped.

'You don't do enough exercise and you eat too much. What did you find for breakfast in the bin today?'

'Oh, not much,' said Rhys. 'There was a slice of pizza with jam, some mouldy cold baked beans and potato peelings, a crust of bread, a dollop of rice pudding, some eggshells . . . oh, and a doughnut with fluff, and cheese . . . at least I think it was cheese!'

'No...no,' said Rhodri. 'That wasn't cheese! That was just very old yoghurt. You had the soft bit; I had the crunchy end which had been in the sun.'

'Eeeukk,' I said. 'That's disgusting! How can you eat like that?'

'You just need a big plate!' said Rhodri. 'It's easy.'

'Or use the dustbin lid,' added Rhys. 'And it saves on the dishes.'

I gave up at that point.

It was Sir Francis Drake from the All Quacks who had the idea. 'If I might make a suggestion,' he quacked, 'why not start to train with us ducks for a while? We have a big game coming up against Bath.'

Well, you should have seen the look on their faces. Rhodri and Rhys were horrified. 'Bath!' they both squeaked. 'BATH!'

Sir Francis shook his beak. 'Not Bath as in soap-and-water bath. The city of Bath. We're playing a team called the Bath Rubber Ducks.'

I couldn't believe my ears. 'The Bath Rubber Ducks?'

'I know, stupid name,' said Sir Francis (of the All Quacks)! 'But a good team, mostly mallards with a couple of Canada geese on the wing.'

Rhodri and Rhys were looking lost. 'What's training?' they squeaked.

Sir Francis puffed out his chest. 'Running, doing circuits and then some more running. Press-ups, sit-ups, squat thrusts and weightlifting.'

Rhodri sat down in the straw. 'Can we join you after a nap?'

Sir Francis folded his wings. 'Be by the pond in five minutes. We're going for a five-mile run.'

I must admit that I had to laugh. Five minutes later, Rhodri and Rhys were out by the pond in some borrowed All-Quack shorts. They didn't look happy. The All Quacks surrounded them and suddenly they were off, with Sir Francis shouting, 'Hup...hup...hup...' for all he was worth and blowing a whistle. Twice round the yard and out through the gates, and then the quacking and whistle-blowing got quieter and quieter until all was peaceful again.

I switched on the radio and relaxed in my straw. Brecon was introducing a competition on *Hoarse FM*, so I sat and listened. All people had to do was to ring in and answer a question. 'What word goes before "horse" and after

"Devon"?' Well, that was easy. The answer was 'shire': '*Shire* horse' and 'Devon*shire*'. I'm a shire horse, and I'm a shire horse with a mobile phone, so I dialled the radio station. Within a matter of minutes I was talking to the lovely Brecon. I must admit I was very nervous.

'So what is the answer, Nelson?' she cooed.

'The…the…the…answer is "horse". I mean "Devon"…No, "shire", Brecon. The answer is "shire". You see I'm a shire horse.'

'In your dreams. Carthorse, more like,' muttered Cardigan from next door. He'd woken up and had stuck his head over the barn door. 'What's happening?'

There was a big fanfare on the radio and Brecon was saying: 'Well done.'

'I've won! I've won…I've won…I've won…!'

'Wow…' said Cardigan. 'What have you won?'

Which was a good question!

'What have I won, Brecon?'

'Oh you are silly,' she said. 'We've been talking about it all morning.'

I was going to tell her that I must have missed it because I had to get a rat out of a drainpipe, but I decided not to.

'You've won a date with me,' she said.

My mouth fell open.

'We are going to the Millennium Stadium in Cardiff and running out onto the pitch with the Welsh Team when they play England next month in the Six Nations. You can bring your friends.'

My mouth stayed open.

'Hello?' said Brecon. 'Hello? . . . Nelson?'

I was absolutely lost for words.

Chapter Three

Half an hour later I was still in shock. Cardigan was trying to talk to me. 'So you're going to the Millennium Stadium?'

'And meeting Brecon,' I reminded him.

'And watching Wales play England,' he said.

'And meeting Brecon,' I reminded him again.

'And running out onto the pitch,' he said. 'What a fantastic thing that will be, running with the Welsh team out onto the pitch.'

My heart jumped and missed a beat. I was thinking. *Running* onto the pitch! Look at me: I can't run onto the pitch. I can't run anywhere. I need to shape up, get fit, have my mane trimmed and have a hoof-i-cure. (That's like a manicure but for hooves.)

Cardigan looked me up and down. 'I think you'd better join Rhodri and Rhys.'

'What?'

'Well, I didn't like to say anything but it's not only the rats who have put on a bit of weight lately. Since you retired and stopped taking regular

exercise, some of that famous muscle has turned to fat. If you want to look your best, you'd better start training as well.'

Suddenly there was a noise in the yard and in fluttered Flight Lieutenant Pigeon.

'They're back,' he said. 'The All Quacks are back, much earlier than usual, but I can't see Rhodri and Rhys.'

I popped my head out. Sir Francis Drake was there, some of the All Quacks were there but I couldn't see any rats. I was about to ask where they were when the gate opened again. In staggered four little ducks. They were carrying Rhodri and Rhys.

Sir Francis closed the gate and ruffled his feathers in a most irritated way. 'I think we need to start again,' he said. 'Something a little easier.'

'How far did you get?' I enquired.

Sir Francis sniffed. 'We've been outside the gate for the last twenty minutes.'

Oh dear. This was not working. I wandered back to my stable for a think.

Flight Lieutenant Pigeon sat on a high perch and watched Cardigan tapping the keyboard of his computer. Cardigan is a very modern horse, despite being very old. He has all the modern gear such as a hayPhone and

hewlett packhorse.

a laptop from Hewlett Packhorse, though he'll soon be upgrading to an iNag 5.

'I like to keep fit,' chirped the pigeon. 'Can't fly if you're not fit, what!'

I nodded. 'You do fly a lot,' I said. 'Mainly in circles...but it keeps you fit.'

You see, the Flight Lieutenant's sense of direction is appalling. Which is how he came to live with us in the first place. He was on his way to France on a top-secret mission. He ended up in Pont-y-cary and he's never left.

He tapped his beak with his wing. 'I've just taken up a new hobby. It's going to get me even fitter. It's called dis-orienteering.'

'Dis-orienteering?'

'Oh yes,' he said. 'You see, it's like orienteering but there is no map and you don't know where you are at the start or the finish...so you can never get lost, can you?'

I scratched my head. 'I don't understand.'

He tried to explain it to me. 'If you don't know where you are in the first place and you don't know where you're going, technically you are never lost. Being lost means you are somewhere you shouldn't be and everybody should be somewhere...'

His voice trailed away. He could see he'd lost me. 'I'm a natural at it,' he continued. 'Everyone at the club says so. There's talk of it being a sport at the Olympics in Berlin in 2015.'

'Brazil,' I corrected him. 'Rio de Janeiro. And it's 2016.'

'Oh, right!' he said, looking a little confused. 'I must mention that to the group. We were going to discuss it at the last meeting but nobody turned up.'

'Where do you hold your meetings?' I enquired, somehow knowing what he was going to say.

'I'm not sure where they're held. I've never found my way back there ... wherever "there" was!'

I let out a big sigh and turned to Cardigan. 'What are you doing?'

'I'm looking for a solution to the Rhodri and Rhys problem,' he said, peering at the screen. 'The jockeys I used to work with attended a gym in Pont-y-cary owned by a fitness fanatic called Morgan Williams. That's how they used to keep fit. I'm looking for a phone number.'

A gym, of course, why didn't I think of that? Cardigan knows lots of jockeys from his time as a racehorse. He was a very good racehorse. Why is he called Cardigan? Because he was a brilliant jumper, of course! Within a matter of minutes, he had found the number he was looking for by going online at 'Oohay' (Flight Lieutenant Pigeon's suggestion: he only thinks it's 'Oohay' because he reads back to front!) and had called the gym. Meanwhile Rhodri and Rhys staggered in and collapsed in the straw.

'I've booked you all in for this afternoon,' said Cardigan, turning off his phone.

'Booked us in where?' panted Rhodri and Rhys.

'We're going to the gym,' I said.

'Which Jim?' asked Rhys.

'Morgan's,' said Cardigan.

'Who is Jim Morgans?'

'No, it's Morgan's gym.' Cardigan was getting a bit fed up.

'Morgan is called Jim?' said Rhys.

'No, Morgan is called Williams,' said Cardigan.

'So who is Jim?' shouted both Rhodri and Rhys.

'No...no...no...' said Cardigan. 'Morgan Williams owns a gym... a gymnasium. It's a place where you can exercise. Look...Morgan used to be called Weighty Williams – he was a bit on the large side. Then he opened a gym, lost loads of weight, got fit and now they call him Williams the Weights. I have just spoken to him and he will see us this afternoon.'

I could see that Rhodri and Rhys were looking anxious. 'Don't worry: the three of us will go together. I need to lose a bit of weight myself,' I said but they didn't cheer up.

'And you can walk there,' said Cardigan. 'It's only in the High Street; the exercise will do you good.'

Two sets of whiskers drooped.

'But we'll have lunch first,' I added.

The rats seemed to perk up a bit. 'There's some of that pizza and jam left,' said Rhys.

'And half a burger still in the box with some melted cheese, a bit of half-chewed bubble gum and an old tube of toothpaste,' added Rhodri, licking his lips. 'You always say we should look after our teeth.'

Cardigan shook his head. 'We'll have fresh fruit, carrots and some spring water.'

'Fresh fruit, carrots and spring water,' they both said. 'That's disgusting!'

Anyway, that afternoon, after a very healthy lunch, we all took a stroll along the High Street. Just beside Mr Evan Evans Bread of Heaven Bakers stood the gymnasium. 'Williams the Weights' owned a big building with pictures on the outside of fit people using running machines, lifting weights and swimming.

Rhodri stared at the pictures. 'Why are all the women wearing giant socks? The men are wearing shorts!'

I sighed. 'Those aren't socks; they're leggings. You need proper sports kit if you want to use a gym...' I stopped myself because I realised that we didn't have any shorts, leggings or indeed giant socks. 'Mmmmmm...We are going to need some proper kit.'

'Oh, what a shame!' said Rhys, nudging his brother. 'We won't be able to go in...isn't that a shame, Rhodri?'

'A terrible shame!' grinned Rhodri. 'And I was so looking forward to wearing a giant rat-sock.'

I held up my hoof for silence. 'Let's find Morgan Williams and ask him if he's got anything that would fit us,' and shoved the two reluctant rats through the doors.

As we walked into the gym, we could see a tall and very fit-looking man in a tracksuit. He had a broad chest and big arms. He strode over to us and introduced himself.

Rhys sniggered. 'He walks like a blaboon!'

'A *blaboon*,' repeated Rhodri and howled with laughter, making monkey noises.

'Shhhh...quiet,' I said. 'That is very rude.'

'Williams the Weights. Pleased to meet you!' Morgan Williams put out his hand and grabbed my hoof. He shook it so hard that I nearly lost a shoe. What a grip! What a shake! Then he did the same to Rhodri and Rhys. They both bounced up and down on the floor as he shook their paws.

'Follow me,' he said and marched off. 'Cardigan thought you would need some gym kit and I have got just the stuff for you.'

Rhodri and Rhys had stopped laughing.

'Cardigan thinks of everything, doesn't he?' said Rhys darkly.

Morgan Williams had gone to a big cupboard in his office and had found two tiny pairs of shorts and two tiny vests.

'Now, what size waist are you, Nelson?'

'Medium,' I said. 'Well, medium to large–ish . . . in horse sizes . . . large, maybe XL if it's a loose fit . . .'

Morgan handed me a pair of shorts and whispered. 'Try XXXXXXXXXXXXL.'

'Thank you,' I said. *'Diolch.'*

'Now, shoes . . . mmmmmm,' Morgan scratched his chin. 'OK, I've got two pairs of 0.001s for the rats and size 54 wides for you, Nelson . . . four of them.'

He handed us the pile of kit. 'Right, that's you sorted. Off to the changing rooms and I will see you in a minute.'

And, with that, he was gone. We stood there for a moment and wondered what was going to happen next.

Chapter Four

Having changed into their gym kit, Rhodri and Rhys were dragging their paws. They really didn't want to go into the gymnasium. I had slipped into my shorts, which were a bit tight, and stood in the doorway with Williams the Weights.

Suddenly Rhys pointed and shouted: 'Look, Rhodri, a tram-bam-po-line.'

'Wow,' said his brother. 'Let's bounce!' and they both shot off across the room.

'No!' I shouted.

'Oh dumb-bells!' said Morgan but it was too late. The rats were leaping up and down, squeaking 'tram-bam-po-line' until the tram-bam-po-line moved and coughed.

'Do you mind?' it grunted.

Rhodri and Rhys jumped off at once.

'I am so sorry, Mrs Hughes,' said Morgan.

Mrs Hughes sniffed, got up off the floor and walked away.

Williams the Weights folded his arms; he was not happy. 'That was no trampoline! That was Mrs Hughes lying down to do her warming-up exercises!'

'Sorry,' said Rhodri. 'But she was so big I thought she was a tram-bam-po-line.'

Rhys started to giggle. 'Mrs Huge.'

'Mrs Huge!' repeated Rhodri and sniggered.

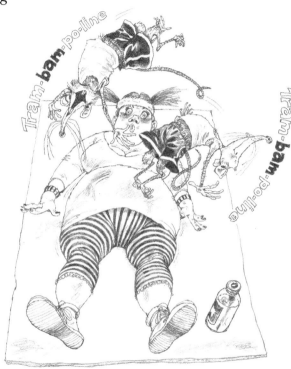

'Mrs Hughes,' I corrected them. 'Now stop that. It is not nice to call people names. Rhodri, you didn't like it when your brother called you a "fat rat". Everybody's different. Some people are bigger than others; some people are thinner; some people look different because they've been in an accident. You wouldn't like it if people called you "dustbin breath", would you?'

They both stood there and twiddled their paws.

'Let's start again,' said Williams the Weights and walked over to a sort of moving-road thing and started showing us how it worked. 'Let's try you on one of these. It's called a treadmill.'

I carefully got onto the machine and waited for Morgan to start it. I looked round for Rhodri and Rhys but couldn't see them anywhere. I looked at Morgan who was staring pointedly at my back.

'Off!' I said and slowly the rats climbed down.

'We thought we could hitch a lift with you,' said Rhys.

'Just for the first couple of miles,' added Rhodri.

'You can use the machine next to this one,' said Morgan and gently picked up the brothers and put them on the treadmill next to mine. 'Now, we'll start you off slowly, at walking pace.' He pressed a few buttons and the floor began to move. I started to walk. Then he did the same to the rats' machine.

'Wooooow,' said Rhys. 'This is weird.'

'I'm walking but going nowhere!' said Rhodri.

After walking nowhere for about five minutes we were all getting a bit bored.

'Can we go a bit faster on the "going nowhere" machine?' asked Rhys.

'If you really want to,' said Morgan and twiddled a few buttons.

The machine speeded up.

I wasn't going to be beaten by a couple of rats so I asked to go a bit faster as well and Morgan adjusted my machine too.

After another five minutes, the rats wanted to go faster again and so did I, so Morgan twiddled. It was at this point that the gym phone rang and he went to answer it.

'How fast can you run, Nelson?' asked Rhys.

'Don't you dare!' I bellowed but it was too late. Rhys had climbed up onto the control panel and pressed a button marked FULL SPEED. I took off! My hooves were a blur. The machine juddered and rattled and bits started to fall off it. The whole gym started to vibrate, and poor Mrs Hughes wobbled like a giant jelly.

All Rhys could do was laugh. He was still laughing when I did a sort of roll and shot off the back of my treadmill. I slid across the floor and hit a water machine. 'Bum! And double bum!'

Rhys looked mischievously across at his brother, who, for once, was concentrating fully on what he was supposed to be doing. Rhys sneaked up onto Rhodri's machine and slowly increased the speed.

'Hang on . . . hang on,' squealed Rhodri. 'Toooooooo fassssssst.'

Rhys was crying with laughter. He thought it was so funny, he had to sit down. Unfortunately he sat on the button marked EMERGENCY STOP. Well, I must say that emergency button was extremely effective. The machine stopped at once . . . but Rhodri didn't.

I never knew that rats could fly! It was lucky that Mrs Hughes was standing there or Rhodri would have shot out of the window. She was just bending down to start her exercise warm-up again when...wallop! You should have heard the scream.

Five minutes later, we found ourselves outside.

Williams the Weights was not a happy man. 'I think it would be best if you did some road work,' he said. 'Out here in the fresh air with my special trainer, Montgomery.'

'Montgomery?' we chorused.

Morgan stood to one side
to reveal a small pig in a red,
white and blue tracksuit.

'Hello,' I said. 'Very nice to
meet you.' I held out a hoof.

Montgomery smiled and
shook it warmly. 'Good to meet
you!'

'May I introduce Rhodri and
Rhys?' I mumbled, pushing
the rats forward.

Rhodri and Rhys just stood there and stared. I knew what the problem was. You see, our new trainer Montgomery was different. Very different. He was short and he was wearing an eyepatch. He only had one ear and when he turned round, we could see that his tail was missing. Around his neck was a whistle, a stopwatch and a gold medal which hung from a long red ribbon.

Montgomery held out his trotter to Rhodri and Rhys. They shook it and then stepped back behind me without a word.

'No time to lose!' grunted Montgomery. 'We shall start with a jog along Brynteg Lane, then into James Street, down Stewart Road and into Caitlin Avenue. OK?'

We all nodded and he was off.

Rhodri and Rhys watched him sprint round the corner.

'Come on,' I said. 'He's getting away.'

'What's wrong with him?' whispered Rhys. 'Montgomery? He's only got one ear . . . and where's his tail?'

'It's none of our business,' I said firmly, 'but I'd guess that he's been in an accident, that's all. There is nothing "wrong" with him . . . in fact he is already halfway down Brynteg Lane . . . so there's nothing wrong with him at all . . . now, come on, before we lose him.'

Well, I never knew pigs could run. He was one fit pig! We tried to keep up as best we could. I'll say one thing for Montgomery: he wasn't too fast but he wasn't too slow either. He did what he called a light 'hog jog'. Every now and again he turned round to help Rhodri and Rhys.

'Pick those paws up. Lift those noses. Get those lungs full of air!'

At the end of Caitlin Avenue, he stopped and let us rest for a while. For me the 'hog jog' was just a gentle trot but for Rhodri and Rhys...well...they were sucking in wind from west Wales. They were pooped but they had made it and I was proud of them.

'Wow,' said Rhys, panting. 'You...are...one...fit...pig. Did you get that gold medal for running?'

Montgomery puffed out his chest. 'Running!' he said. 'Running...I'm the gold-medal marathon winner.'

'Commonwealth Games?' I asked.

'No,' he snorted. 'Olympigs! I represented Wales in the Special Olympigs.'

Chapter Five

Montgomery was a really good trainer. The first week was tough but Rhodri and Rhys stuck with it. They jogged and ran, and watched what they ate...and they ate from a plate as well, not Mike's bin. Montgomery kept checking us to make sure we weren't overdoing things and even I was feeling fitter.

One day, while we were resting at the end of Caitlin Avenue, Rhodri asked a question. 'What happened to you, Montgomery?'

'Shhhh,' I hissed.

'No,' said Montgomery. 'I don't mind telling you. I was in a fire at the farm where I lived. I was lucky to be alive, really. I took a long time to get better and then I decided to get fit and my whole life changed.'

'How did it change?' asked Rhys.

'Well...I really wasn't sure what I was going to do with my life. I used to hang around and feel sorry for myself. Some people used to just stand and stare at me because I looked different. So I decided to go and achieve something...something special. I took up running and I continued to run, run as fast as my little trotters would carry me. Suddenly I was in the Welsh team and off to the Special Olympigs. And I won. But winning wasn't really that important. What was special for me was that I met a lot of great people on the way and did some really interesting things.'

'What? What?' asked the rats.

'Ohhhh...I've taught lots of other animals to run and get fit. I have trained rabbits in "hare-obics". I have turned a lazy lion into a "jog-u-ar" and taught mice to compete in the 400 metre gerbils. I trained meerkats till they were no longer "mere" cats but "super" cats.'

'Wow,' said Rhodri.

'The fire must have hurt,' added Rhys quietly.

'It did,' said Montgomery with a little grunt. 'But I am here to tell the tale, even if I don't have my own tail any more.'

Rhodri and Rhys weren't too sure if they should laugh.

'Don't worry,' grinned Montgomery. 'That's my little joke. But never be afraid to talk to someone if they look different. Some people are rude to me and some people just stare but I'm always happy to talk to anyone. And, look on the bright side, if the fire hadn't happened, I would never have met you two and Nelson, and that would be a shame.'

With that, he was up again and ready for another bit of running. 'Come on,' he said. 'Race you back to the gym.'

Well, I don't mind telling you, after another week or so of training I was feeling pretty good and even looking forward to running out onto the pitch at the Millennium Stadium. It wouldn't be long now before I'd be meeting Brecon, and I could be proud of my new sleek figure since my waist was down to XXXXL! Rhodri and Rhys looked like racing rats and we even beat Montgomery in a race to Caitlin Avenue.

The night before the big match, I was anxious to get to bed early. 'Go to sleep, everyone – we've got a special day tomorrow,' I said as the entire stable settled down. Soon little snores could be heard all around the yard.

Well, it must have been about an hour later that I thought I heard some noises from the direction of Mike's house. And it wasn't snoring. It was James Pond, the lunatic frog. Quite often he goes looking for Russian spies (or is it Russian flies?)...one of the two, anyway, but tonight he was hopping up and down at Mike's back door!

'What are you doing?' I hissed so as not to wake everyone up. 'I know we're all thinking about fitness but do you have to do your workout at this time of night?'

'I'm not doing a workout. Mike was going to watch *Casino Royale* on television. It's the late-night film,' replied James. 'He promised to let me in to watch it with him. But he isn't answering his door.'

'Oh,' I whispered. 'Mike must have nodded off!'

I 'tip-hoofed' over to the window. I could see through the kitchen and into the front room but there was no sign of Mike. Instead, I could see a strange light, a flickering light. 'It must be the television,' I said.

Flight Lieutenant Pigeon fluttered into view, no doubt on his way back from a late-night dis-orienteering expedition. 'Mike's gone to bed,' he said. 'I just flew past his bedroom window and I heard him snoring.'

Odd, I thought. Why had he left the television on downstairs?

By now, Cardigan, the rats and the All Quacks had arrived.

'Shhh, you lot!' I whispered. 'You'll wake everyone.'

'What are you doing?' they all whispered back.

'And why are you whispering?' asked Rhodri.

'Because I don't want to wake everybody up,' I whispered again, and then realised everyone was awake and standing outside Mike's window.

'I don't think that's the television,' said Cardigan slowly as he peered through the back door. 'That flickering light is the fire. And it's getting bigger.'

It was Sir Francis who spoke first. 'I think the front room is on fire.'

'Oh no!' gasped Rhys and Rhodri. Ever since hearing Montgomery's story, they'd been terrified of fire. They'd even wanted to fit a smoke alarm in the stable.

I made a mental note to get Mike to check the smoke alarm in his house. But just then I heard another gasp from Rhys and Rhodri as a flame jumped across the doorway to the kitchen and everyone could see the front-room carpet was well alight. A log from the fire had rolled out. Mike must have forgotten to shut the door of his wood burner before going upstairs to bed.

'What are we going to do?' asked Cardigan.

'I could kick the door down,' I offered.

'The stairs to Mike's bedroom are on the other side of the front room,' said Cardigan. 'It would make no difference. And anyway, the first thing you must do is phone the fire brigade.' And, with that, he cantered back to the stable for his phone.

'We could all shout MIKE,' suggested the All Quacks.

'When Mike is asleep, he is ASLEEP,' I said. 'Nothing will wake him.'

'I'll fly up and peck at his window,' said Flight Lieutenant Pigeon and, in a flurry of feathers, he was gone.

The All Quacks started shouting 'MIKE...MIKE...MIKE...' but nothing happened.

'Come on,' said James Pond. 'This is no good – we have to use our brains! What would Q and M do?'

'Never mind Q and M,' said Rhodri. 'You've got us. Don't use brains, use drains.'

'That's brilliant,' said Rhys. 'And I reckon we'll fit into the pipe now.'

I didn't quite understand till I saw the two rats running over to the drainpipe.

They took one deep sniff and then they disappeared.

Chapter Six

I held my breath and put my ear to the drainpipe. I could hear puffing and panting and scrabbling and scraping. Rhodri and Rhys were climbing up the inside of the drainpipe.

'Where does this come out,' I asked the crowd in the yard.

'Mike's toilet!' said Sir Francis.

'Eeeukk!' I said.

'No, it's just the overflow from the cistern,' he quacked.

'Eeeeeeeeukk!'

It had all gone very quiet. We guessed the rats were climbing higher and higher. James Pond was watching through the window. 'Those flames are getting bigger,' he muttered.

Cardigan came out of the stable. 'I've called the fire brigade. They're on their way. The engine will be here in a couple of minutes.'

I crossed my hooves. A couple of minutes sounded a long time.

Suddenly there was a shout from Flight Lieutenant Pigeon outside Mike's upstairs window. 'Calling Nelson, calling Nelson. Rats on course and target in sight.'

'They're making for Mike's bed,' said Cardigan drily.

We all held our breath.

'Our boys bouncing on target's tummy.'

'I expect Rhys and Rhodri are using Mike as a tram-bam-po-line,' I said. 'He won't be able to stand that for long! Has he woken up yet?'

'No go,' said Flight Lieutenant Pigeon. 'Target still snoring! Rats shouting into both ears.'

'And?' I asked.

'Repeat no go,' said Flight Lieutenant Pigeon. 'Target has moved. Feet sticking out from under blankets. Big toes exposed...'

I held my breath.

'Rats homing in. Teeth bared. They're going to do it. They're really going to do it. They're going to bite him...'

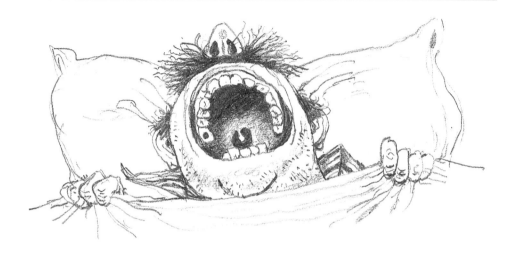

'AAAAAAAAAAAAAAAARGH!'

They could have heard Mike's scream in Cardiff.

'Target awake,' said Flight Lieutenant Pigeon.

'I think we guessed that,' I said. 'Get him to the window!'

After much shouting, squeaking and crashing of furniture, the window flew open.

'WHAT ARE YOU LOT DOING?' roared Mike.

'THE FRONT ROOM IS ON FIRE,' everyone shouted.

'Oh!' said Mike, quietly.

Somewhere, in the distance, we could hear a fire engine. Flight Lieutenant

Pigeon said he could see a blue flashing light but it was a long, long way off. Mike was beginning to cough. Rhodri and Rhys were coughing too and thin wisps of smoke drifted out of the bedroom window.

'We can't use the stairs,' said Mike. 'Look ... Rhodri and Rhys, you slide down the drainpipe and I'll be back in a minute.'

The rats did as they were told and within seconds they were standing in the yard looking back up at the bedroom window. Suddenly a huge white lump appeared. It looked like a giant sausage roll.

The sausage roll got bigger and bigger until it pushed Flight Lieutenant Pigeon off the windowsill. It was then that I realized it was Mike's mattress. 'Catch!' he shouted.

The All Quacks stuck their wings in the air, James Pond held up his flippers and Rhodri and Rhys raised their paws.

Too late.

BAM! The mattress landed on top of them.

There was a lot of quacking and squeaking and croaking, and then everyone reappeared from under the mattress.

'It will break my fall. I'm going to jump,' cried Mike and started to climb out of the window.

'Quick,' I said. 'Everyone grab a bit of the mattress and hold on tightly.'

Well, I know we'd all put on a bit of weight but you try catching a middle-aged milkman in a mattress. It was Mike who should have been on a diet. He hit the mattress like forty crates of 'gold top' with a couple of bags of spuds added. Everyone shot up in the air. For a moment, he was covered in ducks, frogs and rats but thankfully he was safe.

'That was some "skyfall",' said James Pond, picking himself up.

'Not exactly a featherweight, are you?' said Sir Francis Drake.

The flashing blue lights had stopped right outside the dairy and within seconds the sound of boots running across the yard meant that the Pont-y-cary Fire Brigade had arrived. Their hoses made short work of the fire and, in what seemed a very short space of time, Mike was shaking hands with the fire crew and thanking them.

'It's not us you should be thanking,' said the Chief Fire Officer. 'Your friends managed to get you out of the house. They saved your life.'

Mike turned and looked at us. He was still wearing his pyjamas. He had nothing on his feet, his big toes were all red and swollen where the rats had bitten him, but he gave us a great big smile. He scooped up Rhodri and Rhys and hugged them and suddenly we all pushed forward and hugged him back.

'Thank you,' he sniffed, with tears in his eyes. 'What else can I say, but thank you?' And then he stopped.

He sniffed again and looked hard at Rhodri and Rhys. 'You've been in my drainpipe!'

'And through your overflow,' said Rhys.

'And in your toilet,' added Rhodri.

'Eeeeuuuukk,' said Mike. 'Oh, not to worry! Thank you so much for waking me and, let's face it, if you hadn't got fit you wouldn't have been slim enough to climb up the drainpipe or get through my overflow... you two are real heroes.'

'Using Mike's loo as a rescue route reminds me of one of my favourite films,' said James Pond.

'*Towering Inferno*?' asked Rhys.

'No,' said the frog.

'*Waterworld*?' suggested Rhodri.

'No.'

'Well, which film are you thinking of?' I asked.

'*From Flusher with Love*!'

'Yes,' said Mike, sniffing. 'Still, the big question now is: where am I going to sleep tonight?'

'The stable!' I suggested. 'It's warm and dry and as we always say... everyone is welcome.'

It was very late when we settled down. The Pont-y-cary Fire Brigade had to make sure everything was safe and it was nearly morning before Mike had made himself a bed in the straw. Rhodri and Rhys curled up close and put in their earplugs for a good night's sleep. The pigeon went to the rafters, Cardigan to his stall and the frog and the All Quacks back to the reeds.

It seemed only a few hours later when Cardigan's phone woke us up. It was *Hoarse FM*! They had heard of the fire rescue and wanted to talk to us for their news programme.

'*HOARSE FM*!' I shouted. '*HOARSE FM*! Oh yoghurts! Today's my prize day with Brecon. Look at the state of me.' I'd planned to go to 'Hoof-It-Up' the grooming salon, so I could ex-foaliate (well, I was a foal once upon a time), get my hooves done, have a chestnut rinse for my mane and a tint for my tail...

But with the fire rescue and all the mess, I had completely forgotten.

Chapter Seven

As Cardigan spoke to *Hoarse FM*, I had a quick wash, woke the rest of the yard and made sure everyone in the reeds was awake.

'What's happening?' asked one of the little All Quacks.

'We're off to the Millennium Stadium,' I said, checking my mane in the reflection in the pond. 'Quick, the transport will be here in a minute.'

'But we need a proper wash and preen.'

'No time...no time...' I said.

Everyone started to scramble about. Even Mike was up – covered in straw and looking sleepy – but he was up. Rhodri and Rhys licked each other and then offered to give Mike a spit-wash. 'No thank you,' he said politely and went to what was left of his kitchen and used the sink.

The All Quacks splashed in the pond and James sleepily adjusted his bow tie. 'I am shaken but not stirred,' he said and hopped off with muddy flippers, and what looked like a dead fly stuck to his head.

I smoothed my mane down as best I could and then noticed that the All Quacks still had pondweed stuck to them. Mike was dusty and was covered in straw and so was Flight Lieutenant Pigeon. As for Cardigan, well, Cardigan was just Cardigan. He always looks a little battered. I expect I will too when I get to his age. I gave a big sigh. 'That'll have to do. Come on, let's go!'

Within minutes a huge car arrived, all white and gleaming.

'Wow,' said Mike. 'They've sent a Stretch Limo!'

'Wow,' repeated Rhys. 'Did you hear that, Rhodri? They've sent a Stretch Lemon!'

'What?' said Rhodri hopefully. 'A Stretch Lemon? A Stretch Lemon Meringue?'

It was at this point that I asked them to take out their earplugs from last night and everyone piled into the...Stretch Lemon Meringue.

It took some time to get to Cardiff and the streets were packed with people dressed in red. Some wore daffodils and others were dressed as leeks and dragons. Everyone was there to watch the Welsh rugby team. Oh, and some other people had turned up in white shirts with red roses on them but we weren't sure who they were!

Outside the Millennium Stadium we were met by the staff from *Hoarse FM* who showed us the way in. Through the huge gates, across the tarmac, up into the stadium and along corridors. The All Quacks linked wings with Flight Lieutenant Pigeon, so they didn't lose him. Rhodri and Rhys rode on Cardigan's back and James Pond...well James Pond decided to stay with the car. It had a something called a jacuzzi in the back. It was like a giant bath. He hopped in and wouldn't get out. The car company said they would drop him home later, after they'd washed out all the mud.

As we entered the main tunnel to the playing arena, the noise was deafening. I stood at the end of the tunnel looking out onto the pitch. Cardigan squinted over my shoulder. 'Nice bit of grass,' he said. 'We could have a graze at half-time.'

I looked at him in horror.

'Only joking,' he said.

We could see people cheering and the crowds waving flags. In the middle of the pitch was the band of the Welsh Guards. They were playing 'Men of Harlech' and marching around a central figure who was speaking into a microphone...

It was Brecon. She looked lovely.

Suddenly there was a clattering of boots in the tunnel and the Welsh Team arrived. We all shook hands, hooves, wings and paws, and waited.

'We have to stay here for Brecon to introduce us,' said Sam Warburton. 'Then we can all walk out together.'

'Great, everybody's ready,' I said, looking down the line from Cardigan (plus Rhodri and Rhys) to the All Quacks and Flight Lieutenant Pigeon.

'Ladies and Gentlemen,' said Brecon. 'Will you please welcome some very special guests, from the dairy at Pont-y-cary? Put your hands together for Nelson and his friends as they lead out the best rugby team in the world . . . WALES!'

Cameras flashed, music played and the crowd went wild. Off I trotted into the huge stadium, not noticing that Cardigan wasn't behind me. At his age, he's a little slower than us younger horses.

He was ambling down the tunnel at his own pace with the England team stuck behind him.

'Cardigan, you're blocking the tunnel,' said Rhys.

'Let the England team get past,' added Rhodri. 'Move to one side.'

'Yes,' said Rhys. 'Cardigan, pull over!'

But Cardigan plodded on.

When the Welsh team and I reached the centre spot, I looked back to see that everyone else was stuck behind my old friend.

Brecon was now making a second announcement. 'Ladies and Gentlemen, will you please welcome our guests...from England!'

The crowd clapped politely, but there was no sign of the visitors.

Brecon tried again. 'A big hand please...for the English team!'

There was more applause from the crowd but still no visitors. I guessed Cardigan had decided to stop them coming out. I think he was still nursing a grudge from the time someone booed him when he won the Cheltenham Gold Cup. Mike had tried telling him that it wasn't personal, that the man had probably placed a big bet on Cardigan's rival, but it was no good.

Inside the tunnel, Sir Francis Drake, who is an England supporter, had come to a decision. 'Right, All Quacks...one shove should do it...'

Brecon tried making her announcement for the third time. She was beginning to sound panicky. 'Ladies and Gentlemen, will you please welcome our guests...England...'

There was another burst of applause...and then out of the tunnel staggered a very reluctant Cardigan, with the two rats standing to attention on his back, and the All Quacks pushing him from the rear. I guessed they were tickling him. Cardigan is very ticklish, and that's the only way they'd have got him to move. He can be a stubborn old thing.

And right behind Cardigan, fluttering in crazy circles, was a pigeon in a flying helmet.

People started to laugh just as Brecon made her final announcement: 'The English team!'

Cardigan suddenly broke into a canter. The All Quacks shot forward and landed in a cloud of feathers with Flight Lieutenant Pigeon zigzagging wildly after them. I put my hooves over my eyes.

At last the England players managed to squeeze by and run onto the pitch.

Brecon turned and looked at me. 'At last,' she said. 'You must be Nelson,' and she kissed me on the cheek.

My hooves went wobbly. It was then that I looked at the ramshackle gang from Pont-y-cary as they wandered across the pitch.

'I...I...I'm so sorry about that...' I apologised. 'We're all really scruffy. We've had a spot of bother at the dairy.'

'I know,' she said. 'I heard about the fire. But it doesn't matter what you look like. You're safe and you're here and that's the most important thing. Let's find our seats and watch some great rugby.'

And that's exactly what we did. And what a match it was! You're going to ask me who won, aren't you? Well, I've left that till the last page.